The
SURROGATE

L Nicole

THE SURROGATE

Explicit Adult Content Warning

This book is considered erotica and is intended for mature audiences only. This book contains profane language and strong sexual content.

SYNOPSIS

My name is Alejandro Castile but to my clients, I'm Doctor D or Ales. What type of doctor am I? I'm glad you asked. I'm a sex therapist, and my therapy is very hands-on. I work exclusively with women who want to overcome their sexual issues. I use a variety of methods, but mostly, I am a surrogate to help them find their sexual power. A woman who owns her sexual power owns her pleasure, and there is nothing sexier than a confident woman in the bedroom.

Prologue – *Alejandro*

Alejandro, age 16

"Alejandro, come on, we are going to be late to your tia's house."

"Mami! It doesn't matter what time we arrive; they will be partying all night. Why do we have to go so early?"

My mom Anna gives me the death glare, which is my cue to shut up and get a move on. My cousin Wesley is turning 16 today, so the entire family and half of the neighborhood will be there for what will be an all-day all-night party. Don't get me wrong, I'm going to enjoy the party, I just don't want to be there all night.

I'm hanging outside with Wesley and some boys from the neighborhood when this fine ass woman comes through the gate with my uncle Leo and some of his friends. She has to be a woman with the type of curves she's carrying. I track her movements through the yard, and before I can turn away, we lock eyes. She smiles and then turns away. Wesley punches me in the arm to get my attention. I ask him, "Who is that?"

"Oh, that's Maria, and she just moved into the neighborhood."

"So, that's not Leo's woman?"

"No, dude, she's 17, and even he knows he can't touch that." Well, the party just got interesting.

I'm coming out of the bathroom, and Maria is in the hallway talking to some of the girls at the party. We eye fuck each other, and I get bold enough to introduce myself.

"Hi, I'm Alejandro."

She gives me a dazzling smile and introduces herself as Maria. We talk a little bit, but I'm finding it hard to concentrate as she has the sickest body I've ever seen. Where girls my age were slim, Maria has miles and miles of curves. She is 5'5 with long black hair and has pretty brown eyes. Her smile looks like she has a secret to tell you. Her breasts are like ripe melons, more than my hands could fit around. She has long legs and a nice ass. I know I shouldn't be thinking dirty thoughts about a girl I just met, but damn, she is sexy. She grins at me again like she knows what I am thinking.

"Do you have a girlfriend?"

"No," I replied.

"Do you have a boyfriend?"

"No, I don't have a boyfriend. I just moved here a few months ago."

We talk some more and then head back outside to eat. The party is in full swing, and the back yard is packed. Maria and I dance some and decide to go to the front of the house to get some air. I grab her hand as we walk through the gate. Not too many people are milling about upfront.

The sun is going down and a light breeze is blowing. We decide to take a walk to the park down the street.

We arrive and decide to sit on the swings. I'm not going to lie; I want to kiss her and touch those breasts. She must have sensed my thoughts as she got up from the swing and came and stood in front of me.

"Come on, let me show you my secret spot."

I'm not sure what secret spot she is talking about, but I am game to find out. We walk into a thicket of woods away from the park, and lo and behold there is a tree house sitting at the edge of the property.

"I brought you here because I've been wanting to kiss you since I saw you at the party."

"Oh really," I say. "I've been wanting to do more than kiss you."

"Is that right?"

The Surrogate

"Yes," I reply as I step into her face and kiss her lips. Maria wraps her hands around my neck and comes closer. We stand and kiss for what seems like forever, but it's probably minutes. I feel my dick getting hard and start to move away, embarrassed that she got me turned on with just a kiss. Maria gets closer to me, and I feel her lush tits against my chest, and that makes me harder. I'm so turned on I feel like I'm on fire. Maria breaks the kiss. The look on her face is desire as she looks me up and down and stops at the tent in front of my pants. I boldly ask her if she wants it.

She smirks at me and takes off her top. She is standing in front of me in a white lace bra that barely contains her tits. My eyes zero in on her hard nipples, and I lick my lips. My hands are itching to touch them. She pulls her bra straps down then unhooks her bra. Her tits bounce out, all perky with brown nipples that are hard and pointing at me. I just stare like I'm in a trance until she cups them and starts to play with them.

5

I move to her quickly and dip my head to take one in my mouth. I suck gently on the nipple, learning its length and width and how she likes it. When I switch to the other one, I continue teasing the other with my hand. Maria moans and runs her fingers through my hair. I am in heaven and do not want to stop sucking on her bodacious tits. Maria unbuttons her shorts and steps out of them. She pushes my head away and helps me undress until we are both standing in our underwear. I didn't notice a sleeping bag in the corner until Maria starts to unfold it.

"Why do you have a sleeping bag in here?"

"I come here when I want to be alone but sitting on these floors for a long time is uncomfortable, and besides, for what we are about to do, we need some cushion."

"What exactly are we about to do?" I ask.

She takes off her panties and lowers to the sleeping bag.

The Surrogate

"Well, we are about to fuck."

I stand there speechless because I can't believe this is happening and the fact that she is so bold to tell me just that. I am turned on.

"Show me your pussy?"

"Show me your dick?"

Now, I'm not shy about what she is going to see because, well, I'm a dude, and I know my dick is big. I am anxious to get my first feel of pussy. As I step out of my underwear, she looks at my dick, and I'm not sure if the look she is giving me is desire or confusion. A few seconds later, she opens her legs, and I get to see my first pussy. She is not very hairy down there, and when she opens her legs, I see how pink and wet it is. I lick my lips and stroke my dick. It's so hard, and cum is dripping from the head.

"Come here, Alejandro."

I join her on the sleeping bag where we kiss and touch on each other. She grabs my hand and puts my middle finger into her pussy. The sensation of just fingering her pussy and her stroking my dick makes me explode. I cum in her hands. I jump up, embarrassed that I just shot my load from a little kissing and touching. She is sitting on the sleeping bag and starts to laugh. I am so embarrassed and start to apologize. She stands up and walks over to me.

Maria whispers in my ear, "You might be a virgin now, but you won't be when we leave. Now, come back over here. I'm going to teach you how to fuck."

I stand stunned that she still wants to have sex with me. I let her lead me back to the sleeping bag, and we start again. This time when I bust a nut it's in her pussy, and it's the best feeling ever.

We continue to have these fuck sessions for a few months until she meets her boyfriend Juan.

Maria taught me how to eat pussy, how to stroke it, how to tease it, how to make it cum, and since then I've been fascinated with the taste, touch, feel, and smell of pussy.

But enough about me, let's talk about my clients.

The Surrogate

Client 1 – Veronica

Alejandro

My first client is Veronica. She is 5'7, slim with a pair of natural-looking breasts. She has chocolate brown hair hanging to her shoulders. I normally would not have paid attention to her, but this particular evening I do. I'm hanging out at The Lounge having a cocktail and people watching when Veronica and her boyfriend Robbie sit down close to me. I can immediately tell there is some friction happening between them by the distressed look on her face. She is pleading with him when he blatantly tells her she is boring in the bedroom and makes sex a chore. More words are exchanged when she hauls off and slaps him. He probably deserved it. After that exchange, he breaks it off with her and storms out of the place. She starts to gather her things when she notices me watching her.

"Did you enjoy the show? Did you enjoy me being humiliated?" She fires these questions at me with venom.

I smirk and scoot over to her. Up close, she is quite cute with a pair of whiskey-colored slanted eyes. I whisper in her ear, "I can help you with your problem." I slide her my card. "Call me when you are ready to own your pleasure." I kiss her cheek and exit for the night.

Veronica

I arrive at 7:00 pm wearing exactly what he told me to wear, a black dress, black bra, black panties, and my highest of heels.

The Surrogate

Yes, you guessed it, they are black too. As I approach brownstone #27 I feel almost nauseous with the thought of what I'm about to do. The door opens and this man, if he could even be called that, welcomes me. He is 6'2 and ripped everywhere. His voice is warm and deep, and he smells like chocolate. There are no silly pleasantries or small talk as he leads me into this beautiful purple room lit by candles. In the center is the only piece of furniture, an ornate chaise couch. As I look around, he comes behind me and whispers for me to relax. Tonight is all about my pleasure, and I can have as much as I want.

As I exhale, I feel his hands pulling at the tie on my dress. His hands roam from the top of my shoulders to my breasts, my stomach to my thighs. He tells me to take off my dress. I slowly reach to pull it off over my head. He is at my back and quickly unhooks my bra. I start to tremble as I am naked in front of a stranger. Dr. D kisses my neck and brings his hands around to massage my breasts. My nipples harden as I relax into his touch. He removes his hands from my breasts and replaces them with my hands. He gently commands me to continue playing with them. He removes my panties and slides his big hand over my pussy. I still, anticipating him to touch me there, but instead, he slaps my pussy while simultaneously one of his fingers strokes my slit. It was so unexpected and erotic that moan softly. He takes my lips in a crushing kiss and again slaps my pussy. He continues to devour me and tap my pussy. I'm so wet. I want him to slide his fingers inside me, but he stops.

He leads me over to the chaise. He commands me to open my legs and show him my pussy. My legs open just enough to tease him with a peek, but he commands me to spread them and show him all of my pussy. I've never spread my legs so that a man could just see my pussy, but his tone and the look of desire on his face makes me comply. I have my legs spread and he stares at my pussy and licks his lips. I want him to lick me like he just licked his lips. Instead, he commands, "Touch your pussy. Touch it how you want me to."

I slowly slide one finger deep into my pussy and swirl it around, gathering my juices onto my finger. Slowly, I push it in and out.

He says, "That's what you want me to do to you? To barely touch that pretty pussy. You want me to tease it, or do you want me to take it and make you cum?"

I reply, "I can't cum."

He looks me deep in the eyes and says, "You will before you leave here, now, show me how to touch your pussy."

I spread my legs wider and insert two fingers into my pussy and start to roll my hips. I close my eyes, so I don't have to see him watching me. "Eyes open, so you can see what you do to me."

His pants are off, and he is stroking eight inches of the thickest dick I've ever seen. My fingers move faster inside my pussy, making my clit swell. I rub it every time I pull my fingers out. He is stroking his dick in time with my movements, and it's so sexy. I lick my lips when I see his precum on the tip. He knows I want to lick it.

He comes over and stands in front of me. Up close his dick is a masterpiece, and I want to swallow it, bite it, ride it, fuck it. Suddenly, my pussy explodes, and my fingers are drenched. He strokes his dick harder and faster, and then he cums on my breasts. Before I can process that he came on my breasts, he drops to his knees and starts to suck my clit. I grab his head and push him closer. He fucks me with his tongue while inserting two fingers into my pussy. His fingers feel nothing like mine as they stretch my pussy. I moan loudly and play with my breasts. The feeling of his warm cum on my breasts turns me on more. He removes his fingers and sticks his tongue deep inside me. My legs start to shake. I'm moaning so loud and trying to run from his wicked tongue. He grabs my hips, pulling me to the edge of the couch and fucks me with his tongue. I lose my shit and come harder than before. He stands up and rubs his dick across my lips. I eagerly open my mouth to take him to the back of my throat. He moans his appreciation as I squeeze my lips around his head. I suck him harder and faster, liking the sounds he's making. He grabs my head and fucks my mouth until I gag. He pulls out of my mouth and stands me up so that he can take my place on the couch. He says two words, "FUCK ME." So, I did.

See, my problem was that I could never get wet enough to enjoy sex with Robbie. Robbie made me feel like I was frigid and not good at sex, but all it took was one session with Alejandro to bring out my inner sex kitten.

Client 2 – Jasmine

Jasmine

My name is Jasmine, and I don't know why I have talked myself into seeing this Doctor D. I mean, who is he really, and am I really about to get sex lessons from him? Okay, let me clarify my statement. I know how to have sex. I've had plenty of it. I'm just not big on oral sex, giving or receiving. I'm in a relationship with my boyfriend Carlton. We've been dating for almost a year now and everything is perfect, except our sex life. It's kind of predictable, and I know it's my fault because, well, sucking dick is nasty. I've seen it done in porn, and I don't want him cumming in my mouth. What if he smells or I smell funny once we get started? See, that's why I'm here. I want to be able to move past this and blow Carlton's mind.

I arrive at brownstone #27 at noon on Saturday wearing a blue maxi dress and sandals. I ring the doorbell and wait for Doctor D to open the door. I was not ready for 6'2 of a fine ass man. "You must be Jasmine. I'm Doctor D, but you can call me Ales. Please, come in."

He leads me into a purple room that has just one piece of furniture, a beautiful silver and gray ornate chaise. On each wall, there are large mirrors like the ones you find in fancy boutique stores. There are even mirrors on the ceiling. "Why are there so many mirrors?"

"They are for you. I want you to see the pleasure we will give each other. This afternoon we will indulge our senses in sight, touch, taste, and smell. Are you ready to begin?"

I shake my head no as I'm really nervous about doing this with another man. As if he senses my hesitation, he stands in front of me and grabs my hands. "You are here, Jasmine, because you want to please your man, yes?"

"Yes, I say."

"Do you also want to experience the pleasure of receiving?"

"Yes, but…"

"No buts, Jasmine."

He runs his hands over my shoulders and turns me to face one of the mirrors. He stands behind me and unhooks the hook holding my dress together. It pools at my feet. I stand before him in my black half bra and boy shorts. "You have a beautiful body, Jasmine."

His lips are ghosting my neck while his hands stroke my body. He pulls my half bra down and cups my titties in his hands, making my nipples hard. He snakes his right hand down the

21

front of my boy shorts and cups my pussy, rubbing his fingers back and forth. I moan softly and close my eyes.

"No, open your eyes and see what I do to you. See how I'm going to give you pleasure."

I open my eyes and watch as he slides his hand inside my panties. He continues to stroke my pussy with light strokes. Ales slides his leg between mine to spread them wider. He pushes his finger deep into my pussy while pulling my nipple. The sensation makes my pussy clench around his finger. He pulls down my boy shorts and kicks them out of the way. He bites me on the neck and inserts two fingers inside me. I moan loudly and rub my ass against his dick. He pulls out his fingers, and they are glistening with my wetness. He coats his lips with my juices and then licks his lips. "You taste delicious."

He then takes my lips and kisses me so that I can taste myself. I am so caught off guard I have no choice but to taste. He pulls away from the kiss and instead, places my finger and one of his in my pussy.

We stand in front of the mirror and watch as we both create more wetness. He pulls our fingers out, and I protest as I was almost close to an orgasm. He puts my finger in his mouth and licks it. He then takes his finger and puts it in my mouth and says, "Lick it like it's an ice cream cone."

I slowly lick up the sides then swirl my tongue around the tip of his finger. It's so damn sexy, and my pussy is pulsating for more.

"How do you taste?"

"Delicious," I say.

He circles in front of me and drops down to his knees. "Watch me in the mirror."

He places kisses all over my belly and slowly moves down to my pussy. He strokes my clit with his thumb and then spreads my lips. Ales licks me from the back to the front of my pussy with slow deliberate licks. I watch in the mirror and can see every time he flicks his tongue. I am so turned on watching him eat me out. He lifts my right leg and places it on his shoulder. This opens my pussy more, and he goes to town. He's giving me fast strokes with his tongue and rubbing my clit. I try to push him away when I feel my orgasm about to explode, but he just grabs my hips tighter. He stiffens his tongue on my clit, and I explode all over his face and mouth. I scream out my satisfaction while grabbing his hair. He rises from his knees and takes my mouth for another kiss. My juices taste even better.

He leads me to the chaise and spreads my legs. "See how wet that pussy is dripping. You have been denying yourself this pleasure." My pussy is wet and glistening. My clit is standing at attention. We both stare at my pussy in the mirror. I want him to touch it again. He can see the desire in my eyes. He commands me to touch it. He watches me finger my pussy. "Don't be shy; fuck your pussy."

I'm getting close to another orgasm when he drops his shorts and starts to stroke his dick. My fingers still as my eyes take in the sight of his big ass dick. I mean, it's got to be eight inches long, and it's just the right amount of thickness, but that head though. It's massive and currently leaking. He comes and sits next to me on the couch. He takes my left hand and wraps it around the base of his dick, and we stroke it together. I lick my lips as I see more cum leak out of the tip. "Come, Jasmine, come smell my dick."

I get on my knees and lean over to smell him. He smells like chocolate and something spicy. I run my nose up and down his dick and down to his balls. I smell every inch of him. He continues to stroke his dick while I go exploring with my nose. I inhale his scent while gently cupping his balls and stroke his dick.

I'm curious about his taste so I quickly lick his head, so I don't have to think about what I'm doing. He inhales quickly and says, "Do it again."

I take another quick lick and he moans.

"How do I smell?"

"You smell good."

"Taste me." I give him another lick on the head and get more of his salty flavor. His head is calling me, so I wrap my lips around it and give it a suck. He moans, "Fuck yes. Keep doing that."

I take more of him in my mouth, feeling bold and sexy. I continue to suck his head. He smacks my ass and more of his inches fill my mouth. I moan and continue to suck him.

The Surrogate

He strokes my hair, my back, my ass. I want to make him cum but don't know-how. "Jasmine, you're sucking this dick so good. Every time you suck my head, stroke my shaft. I'm going to touch your pussy while you blow me. Look in the mirror and see how you are pleasing me. See how hard I am. You've got me like this. I can't wait to cum."

I feel electricity in my veins as I watch myself take him deep in my mouth. His head is so swollen, and it's leaking more and more. I slurp it up.

I lick his shaft like an ice cream cone and then suction the head just right. He moans louder and tells me to stop or he is going to cum in my mouth. I'm so caught up in sucking that I don't stop fast enough before he starts to cum. I get a little bit in my mouth and on my lips. I watch in fascination as he takes both of our hands and stroke his dick like he is mad at it, but that only makes more cum shoot out. He takes my face and kisses my lips. I kiss him back with a hunger like I've never known. He tastes salty and spicy, and I want to taste more of it.

He breaks the kiss and walks over to a closet where he retrieves a towel. He wipes off his cum and returns to the couch to wipe me down as his cum got on my stomach and legs.

"How do you feel?"

"I feel sexy."

"I like that. You were very sexy giving me head. You take instruction well. Do you have any questions?"

You would think after what just happened, I wouldn't be shy, but I am hesitant to ask.

"What is it?" he says.

"Do you think we can try the 69 position?"

He chuckles and says, "Sure. Do you know what that is?"

"Yes, it's when we do each other at the same time."

"Yes, that is correct. Tell me, Jasmine, why do you want to try that position?"

"Well, when I was sucking you, I wanted to feel your tongue in my pussy at the same time."

"Ah, I see. We certainly can do that, but, Jasmine, don't be afraid to say what you want during sex. If you want to 69, tell him. If you want your ass smacked, tell him. Now, let's assume the position. I'm going to lay down on the bottom and you get on top."

I happily climb on top of him. He pulls me back until I can feel his breath on my pussy lips, and his tongue deep in my pussy. I moan loudly and rotate my hips. He continues to lick me and smack my ass. He stops long enough to give one command, "Suck!" I eagerly take his semi-hard dick in my mouth.

Remembering everything I did before, I go to work. At one point I'm sucking him so good he stops licking my pussy. I raise my head and look back at him and say, "SUCK!" He chuckles lightly and continues to tongue fuck my pussy. His tongue is magical and hitting deep in my pussy. I forgot the mirrors were all around us, and I happen to look, and I can see his face buried in my pussy. He takes his thumb and starts to rub my clit. I lose all focus on his dick as he gives me pleasure. I am mewling like a cat in heat. He smacks my ass, and I go back to sucking, determined to give him as good as he is giving me. I feel his dick swell, and I suck harder. He squeezes my clit while biting my ass cheek, and I explode. I suction his head in my mouth and moan like crazy as my pussy pulses. I guess the vibration of my moans or maybe the pressure of my lips makes him swell even bigger, and he taps my ass to let me know he is about to cum. His cum shoots all over my lips and hands. I lick my lips to taste his essence. I continue to stroke his dick until every last drop flows from the tip, and I kiss his head. He relaxes his grip on my hips and helps me sit up.

"Did that meet your expectations?"

"More than."

"Good, I think you are ready to blow your boyfriend's mind."

Damn right I am. I get cleaned up and leave brownstone #27 with a pep in my step and a devious plan to rock my man's world.

Client 3 – Saraji

Alejandro

I walk into a diner on 25th street and immediately see a petite, cocoa skinned woman with long, jet black hair. I can tell she's a nurse at Saint Helen's by the logoed scrub top. It's a rare Thursday night where I don't have a client and sleep eludes me. I walk to my favorite diner for a slice of pie and hot cocoa. It is mostly empty except for one other couple and her. She is sitting in a booth reading a romance novel. I decide to sit in a booth close to her, so I can study her. It doesn't take long for me to hear her laugh out loud at something she read. Soon, she puts the book down and shakes her head. "Such bullshit." she says.

I know she isn't talking to me, but I answer her anyway. "Totally," I say.

It's then she looks up and realizes that I heard her.

She laughs and says, "Sorry you heard me over here reading this ridiculous romance book."

"Why is it ridiculous?" I ask.

"You know, the usual. The woman is a hot flaming mess and here comes this down to earth, body like a Greek god billionaire to rescue her. Oh, and don't forget, he has a ten-inch penis and gives her multiple orgasms. Yep, that doesn't happen in real life." I laugh with her and ask why she is reading the book if she is so annoyed by it. "Stress relief," she says.

"How is it stress relief?"

"Did you not hear me over here laughing."

"I did."

"May I join you?"

The Surrogate

"Hmm... are you a billionaire with a body like a God and a ten-inch penis?"

Right as she asks me that the waitress comes over with my order, looks me up and down and asks, "Well, are you?"

"One of those things are true, but you have to guess which one."

Saraji and the waitress both say billionaire at the same time. We all share a laugh, and I join Saraji at her table. We are talking for a while when this police officer barges into the diner and heads straight towards our table. Saraji sees him and immediately curses under her breath. She closes her eyes for a brief second and then exhales.

"Who the fuck is this, Saraji? You got off from work over an hour ago and didn't call to let me know you needed a ride." "Malik, this is Alejandro. Alejandro, meet my brother Malik."

Malik and I size each other up before nodding our head at each other. "I didn't call you, Malik, because I am more than capable of getting home, and besides, when I got off from work, I wasn't ready to go home yet."

"Well, I'm here now, and I can take you home," Malik replies.

Saraji

I know it's a moot point to argue with him, so I gathered my things and apologized to Alejandro. I go to put money on the table to pay the tab. He shakes his head. "I got this; it was nice meeting you, Saraji."

The Surrogate

Alejandro - Three months later

I'm at the diner for my usual slice of pie and cocoa when the door chimes and two women enter. I immediately recognize Saraji. She sees me and slides into the other side of my booth saying, "Hey, Mr. Billionaire." I laugh out loud and wait for her to introduce me to her friend. "This is my friend Jacqueline. We work at the hospital together."

"Hello, Jacqueline. It's nice to meet you. I'm Alejandro."

"Oh, it's very nice to meet you."

"What are you ladies up to tonight?"

"Just getting off shift and winding down."

We sit and talk, and sure enough, about an hour later Malik shows up. He stops halfway through the diner, and then I hear a growl. I'm not sure which one of the ladies it's coming from, but they are not pleased to see him. He notices me.

"You again? Are you stalking my sister or my wife?"

Before I can respond, Jacqueline jumps up from the table and gets in his face. "I am not your wife. You haven't put a ring on this finger."

"I did put a ring on that finger and this dick all on that ass. You are mine, Jackie."

Come on, Alejandro, let's go because these two are just going to argue for the rest of the night.

"Well hello to you to, Saraji."

"Whatever, Malik."

We grab our things and leave money on the table for the tab.

"Do you live near here?" asks Saraji.

"Yes, I live two blocks up."

The Surrogate

"Where do you live?"

"I live on 10th and Howard. I only come to the diner because it's close to the hospital."

"How about we go to my place, and I'll get my car and take you home?"

"You don't have to do that. I'm sure I can go break them up, and Malik will take me home."

We both glance back into the diner to see Malik and Jacqueline still sitting in the booth arguing.

"Listen, Saraji, it's no problem to take you home."

"Thank you, Alejandro, I would like that."

We walk the two blocks to my brownstone. My car is parked in the back. I unlock the door to the house so that we can go in and out the back without having to walk around the corner to the alleyway. Saraji is a little hesitant to enter.

"What is it?"

"You're not a crazy psycho, are you?"

"No, I'm not. I'm a harmless therapist just trying to see that a beautiful woman makes it home safe."

She smiles shyly. Saraji comes inside and follows me from the foyer when all of a sudden, I hear her gasp. I turn to see that she is not behind me but has stopped inside the doorway of the purple room.

"You like my couch?" I ask with a smile in my voice.

"That is the most beautiful couch I've ever seen, but what's with all the mirrors?"

"They are for therapy of sorts."

"Therapy? What kind of therapy?"

"Sex therapy."

The Surrogate

She turns to me with a look of astonishment. "You're a sex therapist."

"Yes. I can help you."

"I'm not so sure of that."

"I'm sure of it, Saraji."

"How do the mirrors help?"

"Now, I can't tell you my secrets unless you become my client." I can tell she is curious, but she is also stubborn and doesn't want to accept that she needs help with sex. "Come on, let me take you home."

L. NICOLE

Saraji - Two months later

I can't believe I am here for sex. I haven't had sex in three years since my attack. The thought of being penetrated makes my skin crawl. I have worn the hell out of my rabbit for that simple reason. I want to get past this, so I can start dating. I would like to be in a relationship again and don't want to bring this baggage into it. I ring the doorbell, and Alejandro answers it like he's been expecting me. He has actually. I've been standing on his stoop for fifteen minutes mentally hyping myself up to do this.

"Come in, Saraji."

I enter and stand inside the foyer. He grabs my hand and leads me into the purple room. The room is lit up with candles of all shapes and sizes. A calming scent of lavender and citrus envelops me. There is a beautiful chandler hanging from the ceiling and more mirrors. I bet they are a bitch to clean.

We sit on the chaise, and he turns towards me. "Saraji, you are safe here. We only go as far as you want to go. We only go as fast as you want to go. Do you understand?"

"Yes," I say with a stutter in my voice. He lifts my chin and stares into my eyes. I notice his eyes are light gray. He leans in and kisses me softly on the lips. I return his kiss just as softly. Suddenly, I feel myself being pulled forward into his lap. We continue to kiss, while his hands rub my shoulders and down my back. I rub my hands down his chest. He feels so solid and warm. He smells like melted chocolate and something spicy. I want to bury my nose in his neck and just inhale. Anxious to feel his skin, I run my hands under his shirt. His stomach is flat but not rock hard. I caress his chest. He breaks the kiss to take off his shirt. I plant kisses on the sides of his neck and

43

down this throat. I run my tongue along his Adam's apple and back up to his lips. We kiss hungrily, and I angle my head to get more of his lips and tongue. I feel his hard dick pressing against my ass, so I grind on it. Alejandro runs his hands down my back and then from my stomach to my breasts. He stills his hands and asks in a husky breath if he can touch them. I ache to feel his hands on them. I can feel my nipples poking through my bra. He takes his thumbs and rubs them across my nipples, making them longer and harder. My panties are getting wet from feeling his long length against my ass. I slide my dress off my shoulders. He kisses my neck, down to the tops of my breasts. He bites me gently while slowly removing the straps.

"I want to see and taste your breasts. Take off your bra and feed me."

I slide the bra off and lift my 38 C's to his waiting mouth as an offering. He massages my breasts before sucking the right one into his mouth. His tongue is electric. It feels like he is sucking and pulling at the same time. I close my eyes and enjoy the way he is devouring me. He takes turns going between them. I push his head further between my breasts while raking my nails through his hair. He lets out a sexy moan that makes my pussy clench. My pussy is throbbing, and I want more. I want more from him, so I stand up and pull my dress down to where it pools at my feet. I'm in my panties and heels, and the way he is staring at me makes me feel sexy. He pulls me closer to him and puts his face in front of my pussy and starts to sniff me, taking deep breaths of my scent. I get a little nervous and start to pull away. He gently grabs my hips to keep me still so he can continue to torture me with anticipation of what he is going to do. He looks into my eyes and asks if he can see it. I answer yes, and he slowly pulls my purple lace panties down my legs where they meet my dress in a puddle. "I'm going to taste you now."

I watch as he glides his tongue between my pussy lips. The first touch of his tongue makes me jump a little. "Don't worry, I got you. If you don't like it, tell me. If you want me to stop, tell me, and I will. You smell like strawberries, and I want to taste your flavor all night." He grabs my hips and slides his tongue back inside me. I want to watch, but I can't help but to close my eyes and get lost in the bliss that he is providing. I'm moaning so loud and stroking and pulling my rock-hard nipples. I'm so close to cumming. He picks me up and places me on my back on the couch. He puts my right leg over his shoulder and continues to eat my pussy like it's his last meal. I fuck his face. "Oh my God, don't stop. Don't stop," I whisper moan. He flicks his tongue over my clit, and I cum so hard. My legs are shaking, and I don't know what I'm saying, but he gets the point. His tongue is fucking magical.

The Surrogate

I lay there spent when I feel him move away from my pussy. He covers my body and comes up for a kiss. I taste myself on his tongue, and I want more. He raises and starts to undress. I take in the sight of his beautiful body. He has tattoos covering his upper chest and nice abs that I want to explore with my fingertips and tongue. He has thick thighs and nice toned legs, even his toenails are sexy. I'm not going to lie, I gawk at him like he is on display at the national museum of sexy men. His dick is nice and long. I freeze up looking at it, and thinking about it being inside me makes me hyperventilate.

"Saraji, look at my face. Look at me. I'm not going to hurt you. We don't have to fuck tonight. We can do whatever you want. Remember, it's me and you, no one else. No one is going to give you pleasure tonight but me."

I stare into his gray eyes. I shake my head and say yes to give my consent.

47

He pulls me up from the couch, and I wrap my arms around his neck while we kiss. He grabs my ass and squeezes it while nibbling on my neck. I reach down and stroke his dick. It's so hot and heavy in my hand. I relish stroking him and lose myself in the up and down motion of my hand moving over his shaft, feeling the cum ooze out of the tip. I love hearing him breathe harder as I grip him tighter. I'm so caught up that I'm not aware that he has slid a finger in my pussy. I'm so wet, and his finger is stirring the pot. He dips his head to take my breast into his mouth. His thumb is pressing against my clit while he moves his finger deeper into my pussy. Only when he adds another one do I start to panic. He stills his finger and tells me to look at him. I open my eyes and look at him. While I'm looking at him, he slowly starts his movements. With slow and shallow strokes, he works my pussy. I'm moaning, and my hips start to move with his fingers. "That's it, baby, fuck my fingers."

The Surrogate

We stand there kissing with me grinding on his fingers. He pushes deeper into my pussy, and it clenches around his fingers. I'm so close to cumming again. My pussy is so wet, it's starting to leak. He rubs my clit faster and pumps his fingers harder and faster inside me. I cum so hard, and yell so loud, it's a wonder the mirrors didn't break. I grab his shoulders to hold me up for support as I ride his fingers through the very last tremors of my pussy.

He lays us on the couch with me on top. He strokes my hair and rubs my back. "I think that is enough for tonight. I don't want to push you too far."

My body is so relaxed and languid. I raise my head and look at him. "What about you? I can still feel how hard you are."

"Don't worry about me."

"Tonight was about getting you comfortable with being touched and tasted."

It seems like a damn shame to let that dick go to waste. I know he said he doesn't want to rush, but that doesn't mean I couldn't taste him. I slide down his body and get on all fours over his dick. I slowly take his thick head into my mouth and suck. He bites his lip while watching me swirl my tongue over the head before putting it between my lips. I stroke his shaft as my lips and tongue work the head. His eyes are closed while I work that dick. I suck and lick until I feel more precum leak from the head. I want to fuck him so bad. I reach between my legs and start to rub my clit. Oh shit, he moans as he watches what I'm doing. He grips my hair and growls when I take as much of him as I can in my mouth. I'm close to cumming again when I feel him start to pull away. I put my hands on his thighs and suck him faster. He yells, "I'm about to cum."

The Surrogate

He's so deep in my mouth that most of his cum goes down my throat. Feeling him cum makes me cum again. His dick plops from my mouth, and I wipe my lips with the back of my hand. "Damn, that was good," he breathes out. "Thank you for getting me off." I smile at him, showing all my teeth like I just won a prize. We take a moment to collect ourselves and get dressed. He walks me to the door.

"Your homework is to buy a dildo in any size you think you can handle. I want you to practice masturbating with it. If it's too much or makes you feel uncomfortable then pleasure yourself with your fingers. As many fingers as you can handle." I don't know what made me blush more with embarrassment, this handsome man telling me to buy a dildo or to fuck myself. "Do you understand?"

"I don't, actually, but if you think that's next, then okay."

"I want you to get use to penetration."

"So does this mean you're not going to have sex with me?"

"Oh, I plan on having sex with you, but we must do this first."

He kisses me lightly on the lips. "I'll see you in three weeks."

I ended up working overtime at the hospital, so it was more like four weeks before I could see Dr. D again. I wasn't as apprehensive this time. Just thinking about our last session gets me turned on. I don't know if we will have sex this time, but I'm ready to find out. I ring the bell, and Alejandro greets me with a kiss on the cheek. He is wearing a light blue Polo dress shirt with gray slacks. The black belt and shoes pull his look together. I've never seen him this dressed up. He looks and smells delicious.

"Hello, Saraji. You look lovely."

The Surrogate

He grabs my hand and leads me past the purple room. "We aren't using the purple room tonight?"

"No, not tonight. Tonight, we need a bed."

He leads me down the hall and into a beautiful blue room. The walls are navy blue. The windows are covered with white and silver silk curtains. The bed is a huge king size canopy bed made of dark wood. Next to the window are two huge silver chairs with a low table in the middle. I take all of this in while Dr. D lights the huge fireplace. The room becomes nice and cozy and casts the room in shadows. He turns on the lamps next to the bed so there is more light. "Come here, Saraji."

I join him near the bed where he grabs me and kisses me passionately on the lips. I wasn't quite ready for the kiss but relaxed into his arms and let him thoroughly taste every inch of my mouth. I wrap my hands around his neck and fuse my body to his. The heat from his body and the licks of his tongue across my lips sends my body into overdrive.

He lifts the hem of my dress and bunches the fabric around my waist. He grabs my ass and pulls me closer so I can feel the hardening of his dick. "Take off your dress," he commands. I whip the dress off before he can blink.

I'm standing in front of him in a sheer purple bra and thong. Before you even ask, yes, I bought them specifically for this appointment. He looks at me through low hooded eyes. Turn around and grab the post. I feel his body heat against my back and lean toward it. He runs his hands across my stomach and up to my breasts while biting my ear lobe. I feel him unhook my bra, and my breasts spill out. He palms them into his hands and rolls my nipples. I moan and arch my ass into his dick.

The Surrogate

He continues to play with my nipples. He takes my right hand from the post and places it on his dick. I stroke him through his pants. He is so long, and I feel his dick getting harder the more I play with it. Sliding my panties to the side he glides a finger against my pussy lips before inserting one long finger. I freeze when I fill his finger inside of me. He whispers in my ear, "Relax, it's me touching you."

I turn my head to capture his lips in a searing kiss. He slides his finger in and out of me before he stops and removes my thong. He kisses my ass cheeks and up my spine. He kisses my neck and slides his finger back inside my aching pussy. He continues to stroke my pussy, now adding his thumb to stroke my clit. I shamelessly grind against him. I close my eyes and give in to the feeling his masterful fingers are creating. He squeezes my breasts, and I come apart on his fingers.   He turns me around, and my eyes immediately go to the bulge in his pants. "Undress me."

I step to him and unbutton his shirt. Next comcs his pants and boxer briefs. Seeing that dick up close like this makes me lick my lips. I finish undressing him and wrap my hand around the shaft of his dick. It's so warm and thick.

"Did you bring your toy?"

"Yes, but I don't want that when I can have this."

His laugh is dark and deep. "We will see IF you will get this. Now, get your toy." I walk over to the chair and reach inside my purse to pull out the dildo. He takes a look at the rather modest-sized toy then brings it to his nose to sniff it.

"You haven't used it."

I blanch at his accurate assessment and feel my face getting hot. I sorta kinda used it, but I wanted the real thing.

"Why didn't you use your toy?"

"I started to use it, but it didn't feel real, so I used my fingers most of the time."

"Tell me, how many times did you use your fingers to pleasure yourself?" I look away from him and say five.

He grabs my chin so that I am facing him. "There is nothing wrong about pleasuring yourself five times. Some people do it every day. You did what felt good to you. Okay?"

"Okay," I say. He gives me another one of his drugging kisses.

He picks me up and places me in the middle of the bed near the headboard. He kisses down my body and spreads my legs wide. Show me how you touched yourself. I look into his gray eyes and slide a finger into my pussy. I'm so hot and wet. A moan escapes my lips as I stroke my pussy. Knowing he is watching turns me on more, and I slide another finger in. He leans over and sucks my nipple into his mouth. I grind my hips and fuck my fingers harder. I feel his finger slide in with mine, stretching me. He pushes our fingers deeper into my pussy. I scream, "Oh shit," and my back arches off the bed.

"Your pussy is so hot and tight." he breathes out next to my ear. He rubs his thumb against my clit in fast circles while my pussy clenches around our fingers. I'm so close to cumming.

"Relax, baby, and let it happen."

I can feel my pussy dripping. He bites my nipple and presses his thumb into my clit, and I detonate. I feel my pussy gushing. My legs are shaking. My eyes are closed, and I see nothing but stars. I open my eyes when I feel something pressing against my pussy lips. Dr. D has the dildo, and he is running it lightly against my entrance. He pulls it away and brings it towards my mouth. "Suck it; get it wet." He places the dildo on my lips, and I open my mouth to suck the head. He pops it out of my mouth and opens my legs. He runs the dildo against my entrance, and I brace for him to push it in.

"Tell me what you are thinking? Why are you tensing up?"

"It's been a while, and the last time it happened wasn't a pleasant experience."

"Let's change that. Do you trust me?"

"Yes."

"Do you trust that I want to pleasure you and not hurt you?"

"Yes."

He leans over me, and we kiss. "Touch me," he commands.

I touch every part of him I can reach ending with my hand around his thick dick. He takes my hand and has me gripping him tighter and stroking faster. I'm so engrossed with stroking his hot velvet dick that I don't see the dildo coming. He slowly pushes it inside my pussy and pulls it back out to the entrance. He repeats this until I start to slowly moving my hips. He spreads my pussy lips and slides the toy in deeper. I tense again, not expecting it to be so far inside me. He moves it slowly in but not all the way out. "You look so sexy. I wish it was my dick sliding inside you right now."

I moan because I want that too. "Look at the ceiling and see how hard you have my dick. See how I move this inside your pussy, how it clenches for me."

The Surrogate

I'm so turned on and move my hips faster. He speeds up the thrusting into my pussy, turning the toy inside my pussy so that it rubs my walls then pushes it deeper. I spread my legs wider so I can watch how he fucks me with the toy. I massage my breasts and tweak my nipples. I'm moaning every time he pushes it inside my pussy. I hear him breathing hard against my ear as he works every inch of the toy into my pussy. He leans down and continues to fuck me with dildo in one hand and rubs my clit with the other. A few strokes and I scream my release. My pussy is dripping all over the sheets. He continues to move the dildo inside me, making me moan until the tremors stop. He removes the dildo from my pussy and puts it in my mouth so that I can taste myself. I am so spent, I can barely move.

"Are you okay, Saraji?"

"Yes, I'm fine. I feel like a cooked noodle."

"Well, then, mission accomplished, as I wanted you to be a limp noodle tonight."

We laugh and lay on the bed for a few minutes.

Alejandro

After making Saraji cum with the dildo I am contemplating pushing her limits to see if she can handle it again. She makes the decision easy for me when I feel her hands stroking my dick. I let her stroke me before I remove her hand. "Stand up on the bed and hold onto the headboard."

She looks at me with curiosity. Once she is standing at the head of the bed facing me, I spread her legs apart and place a kiss to her clit. I flick my tongue into her hot channel. She is so fucking wet. I tongue fuck her hard and fast. She holds my head to her pussy and chants, "Oh oh oh," with each flick of my tongue. Instead of giving her my fingers to fuck I slide the dildo into her pussy and fuck her with it. I suck her clit and circle her pussy with the toy. I grab my dick with my left hand and stroke it fast in time with the movement of the dildo inside her pussy. She is dripping, and close to cumming, from the way she has a grip on my hair and the headboard. A few more pushes deep inside her channel sets her off, and she cums hard and loud. Her pussy grips the dildo, and I stand to my feet still stroking my dick. I squeeze the head harder each time I stroke from the shaft to the head. I am close to coming when she drops to her knees. She takes my head into her mouth and flicks her tongue all around it then slides me deeper into her mouth. She is sucking me and stroking the few inches she can't get down her throat. I encourage her efforts by stroking her hair. Her mouth feels fucking amazing. She reaches down and strokes my balls with the pad of her hand. That shit makes my legs tremble a little bit. She sucks me harder until I cum down her throat, taking every drop of my cum. I grab the headboard to keep my balance until she removes my dick from her mouth. We both slide back down to the bed and look at each other in the mirror on the ceiling. We wear twin expressions of satisfaction. After a while, we get out of bed and get dressed.

"Saraji, I am really proud of you tonight. You didn't tense up at all on the second go round."

She blushes lightly.

"How do you feel?"

"I feel like a very satisfied noodle."

I kiss her on the cheek. "I'll see you in a few weeks for the final session." I see the Uber pull up and walk her out to the car.

The Surrogate

Tonight was a good session indeed. I can't wait to see how she takes my dick.

Saraji - One month later

I have been on pins and needles for this appointment. This is my last one, and I hope that I can handle him. I've used the dildo twice, but it's a poor substitute for what he's packing. I arrive at his place at 7:00 pm. He opens the door wearing blue basketball shorts and that's it. I am captivated by his beautiful tan skin. I want to lick every inch of him. I guess he asked me a question, and now he is looking at me like I'm a weirdo. "Are you okay, Saraji?"

"Um, yes."

"Come," he says as he takes my hand and leads me to the blue room. It is set up just the way

I remember, except tonight, I smell a subtle fragrance of vanilla.

"Tonight, with your permission, I would like to give you a pleasurable experience." My body heats up at the thought of finally having sex with him. "Take off your clothes and get in the middle of the bed." He watches as I take off my shoes then my black skirt and silk cranberry sleeveless top. I unclasp my black lace bra and wiggle out the matching panties. He looks at me like he is starving and I'm his last meal. I hop up on the bed and crawl to the center, making sure he sees all my goods. By the smirk on his face, he saw it and knows what to do with it. I watch as he removes his shorts. His dick is at attention as he slowly strokes it while looking at me. I lick my lips in anticipation, but he just stands there stroking his dick. Slowly, he makes his way to the bed, and his body covers me. He leans on his elbows and presses his chest into mine while taking my lips in a searing kiss. We kiss passionately. Our tongues meet and collide. I stroke his back and chest while trying to wrap my legs around his waist. He kisses my neck and collarbone down to the tops of my breasts. He takes my right nipple into his mouth and makes the tip harder, then he switches to the left. He is massaging my breasts, and his thumbs tease my nipples. He pushes my breasts together and hungrily kisses, bites, and sucks every inch of them. I moan as I have never had my breasts played with like this. My pussy is throbbing when he releases my breasts and kisses his way down my stomach. He leans back on his knees and caresses my legs up to my thighs. He massages the inside of my thighs while pulling them apart.

"You have a beautiful pussy. Can I taste it?"

I spread my legs further to allow him full access. He leans over and places kisses on my mound before sliding his tongue into my hot pussy. The first touch of his tongue is ecstasy as he slides it back and forth, up and down my lips. He makes my pussy drip like a faucet. His lips find my clit, and he vibrates his tongue over it. I grab his head and fuck his face. "Ales, just like that. Just like that."

He hums his pleasure and pins my knees to the bed, spreading me like a butterfly. He pushes two fingers inside my tunnel, and I cum. My pussy gushes so much I feel it on my thighs.

Ales climbs back up my body and we kiss. He rolls us so that I am on top of him. I kiss him from his lips down to his navel. His dick is hard and standing at attention. I lick the head of his dick and taste the cum that spills out of the top. I lick up and down his shaft, making it glisten. I put my lips to his dick and suck him fast, slurping, gagging trying to get all of it in my mouth. He moans his approval by grabbing my head and fucking my mouth.

The Surrogate

"Play with that pussy while you suck me." I reach down and rub my pussy. My fingers can barely stay inside me, I'm so wet. I suction his head when he suddenly pulls out of my mouth. "I have to have you right now, Saraji." He reaches under a pillow and pulls out a condom quickly sheathing his dick. He lifts me and lines his dick up to the entrance of my dripping pussy. He looks me in the eyes and pulls me down on his dick. I scream from the sensation of being so full and stretched. I try to get off him and get it out of me at the same time. He pulls out and stills my hips as I try to leave from off top of him. The dildo did not prepare me for that.

"Saraji, look at me. Open your eyes and look at me." His voice is a gentle command. I open my eyes and look at him.

"You can handle me, Saraji, every inch a little at a time. I won't hurt you. When you are ready, take my dick."

He rubs my shoulders and breasts. He places little kisses on my lips and neck. I try to calm my nerves, but then he takes my nipples into his hot mouth and sucks. My pussy is so wet. I inch up so I can slide down on his waiting dick. I keep my eyes open and on his face. His dick is so hard and stretches my walls. I don't know how much I've taken, but he stills all movement between us so I can adjust to him. I start to move slowly up and down his length. The look on his face is that of exquisite torture. His breaths are short rapid pants every time I slide up and down. He feels so good. I speed up the movements of my hips taking more of him until he is seated deep in my pussy. "Oh my God", I pant between sliding down on his dick again and again. He whispers my name while gripping my hips. He does not move. Letting me control the tempo. I pick up the pace and all types of gibberish flows from my mouth. Ales smacks my ass and encourages me to ride his dick. He moves his hand down and finds my clit. His ministrations make me grip him tighter.

"Fuck!" He yells and continues to play with my clit. I can feel my orgasm building when he starts to pump into me. I lean back and place my hand on his thigh so he can continue rubbing my clit. "Oh shit... oh shit... I'm so close. Please, Ales."

He leans up and bites the underside of my breast, and I cum. I scream. I moan. I have an out-of-body experience as surely my soul has left my body.

Alejandro

Saraji's pussy is gripping the fuck out of my dick. She is riding me hard and fast now. I can't wait to feel her cum. Her eyes are closed, and all

I hear is oh shit, oh shit. I feel her pussy dripping down my dick to my balls. I squeeze her hips and bring her mouth down to mine for a kiss. I roll us over so that I'm on top. I slide my dick into her trembling pussy and give her slow strokes filling her tight pussy to the hilt.

She moans and rolls her hips to take me.

"Can I fuck you harder, baby?"

"Yes, please, give it to me."

I speed up the tempo and raise her left leg up to my shoulder so I can go deeper. I feel her nails in my back. I love that shit. I rotate my hips and push deeper into her pussy. Fucking her harder until every inch is inside her. "That's it, baby, you're taking all this dick." All I hear are her moans, yells of pleasure, and the slap of my balls against her pussy. "Ales! Ales! Please, I can't take anymore." Her legs are shaking, and her pussy has a death grip on my dick. "Do you want me to stop?" I ask as I swivel my hips and hit her deep.

The Surrogate

"I... I... FUCK!" Her body tenses as she cums. Her right leg wrapped around my waist, has me pulled tight against her body. I let her leg down and continue to stroke her pussy. I'm close to cumming, so I pick up the pace. I feel her nails scratching my back and then my ass. My dick swells, and I cum on a powerful stroke deep inside her pussy. My orgasm is long as I fill the condom with my seed. I take her lips in a hard kiss. I slide out of her, and we both moan at the loss of that heat. I get out of the bed and go to the bathroom to remove the condom and get a wash towel. When I return to the room, Saraji is crying into the pillow. I ease up on the bed and stroke her back.

"Saraji, what is it? Did I hurt you?"

She turns her head to look at me through teary eyes. "You didn't hurt me, you helped me. You probably broke my pussy, but, no, you didn't hurt me." I wipe the tears rolling down her face and kiss her lips. We continue to kiss softly as I gently caress her body until we eventually fall asleep.

Client 4 – Yara

Alejandro

It's not often that I am contacted by husbands or boyfriends for help with their significant others, especially about sex, but that is exactly what happened when Adam Phillips contacted me about the problem he is having with his wife Yara. He loves her but does not want to divorce her just because she sucks the fun out of sex. He complains that she treats their sex life like it's another thing on her to-do list. She does not enjoy it, and she is just doing it because she knows he wants to have sex. I am intrigued and also baffled as to how he expects me to help her. I agree to meet with them so I can get a better understanding of what is happening in the marriage and if my particular brand of therapy will help.

Adam and Yara arrive at my office at 3:45 pm. I am struck by how beautiful Yara is. She is 5'8, cafe au lait complexion with striking green eyes. Her hair hangs down her back like miles and miles of silk. She is wearing a gray herringbone dress that shows off her tiny waist and wide hips. She looks as if she stepped out of a board meeting. The look on her face says she would rather be anywhere else than here. Adam is not a bad looking guy. He is also 5'8, slim but fit. He has black hair and blue eyes. His face is one of frustration.

The meeting does not go well. Adam is not the calm and concerned guy that he made himself out to be on the phone. He started the meeting by being a real dick. Let me see if I can sum up his words to Yara. "Yeah, we are here so this guy can help you stop being a frigid bitch in bed so I can enjoy sex with you." As you can imagine Yara did not respond well.

The Surrogate

Her exact words, "Maybe, he can help you be a better lover then I would enjoy it, you arrogant asshole." Que the dramatic exit with a door slam. Adam rushes out after her. Needless to say, they did not return.

Alejandro - Six months later

I'm running late for dinner with my friends at Salvants. It's not like me to be late, but my last client appointment went a little longer than usual, but in the end, she was sexually satisfied and happy. I arrive at Salvants and I'm taken to the table where my friends have just been seated. We are enjoying drinks and appetizers when I feel like someone is staring at me. I glance around and lock eyes with Yara. I am surprised to see her but make no move to go over to her table. She breaks eye contact with me when one of the ladies at her table gains her attention. I periodically steal glances at her throughout the evening. She is fucking beautiful. Her face transforms into something angelic when she smiles. You know how Julia Roberts is pretty, but she is gorgeous when she smiles. Yeah, that's how Yara is. I truly wonder if she is frigid in bed, or is her husband just being a dick. It would be unprofessional of me to finesse her to find out, so I leave that thought alone.

I leave the restaurant hours later, and while waiting on valet to bring my car, Yara approaches me. I don't know if you remember me or not, but my husband Adam and I came to your office some months ago. "Yes, I remember. You two were my most interesting appointment that day." She looks away while color tinted her cheeks. "Well, we are not together anymore. Seems like that appointment was the last chance for our marriage."

The Surrogate

"I'm sorry to hear that."

She turns her head to look at me, and her eyes are shining with unshed tears. "Are the things I hear about you being able to help women with problems really true?"

"It depends on what you are hearing," I say with a smile. She smiles back. The valet returns with my car, so I hand her my card. Call me when you are ready.

Yara - Two months later

I arrive at brownstone #27 at 4:00 pm. I rearranged my schedule to make sure I could make it on time. He said to clear at least three hours for this session. Three hours? I can't imagine what we are going to do for three hours, but I guess I'm about to find out. I ring the doorbell, and Doctor D opens the door wearing the hell out of a navy-blue suit. The suit has to be custom because it is fitting his body like a glove. He is wearing a blue patterned shirt with the top two buttons undone and no tie. He looks sexy, and he smells like sin. Just smelling him makes my mouth water. He leads me past a gorgeous purple room with lots of mirrors. He opens a door into what looks like a small spa room. "We are going to start this afternoon with a massage. Please take off all your clothes and lay on the table face down. I'm going to change and will be back in a few minutes."

I look at him with a raised eyebrow. "I wasn't expecting this. I thought we would talk and then have sex."

"We will see where our time together takes us. Now, get naked. I'll be back in a few minutes."

When he leaves the room, I hesitate to undress. My need to know what's going to happen, to know the rules of engagement paralyze me. I want to leave, but then I hear Adam's voice degrading me. I strip and get on top of the comfortable massage table. It's then I realize that there is no sheet or gown to cover me. I start to feel nervous about him seeing my body and not knowing what he is going to do. I hop off the table just as Doctor D comes back into the room. I grab my dress and place it in front of my body to shield my nakedness from him. He notices the flush on my cheeks.

"What's wrong?"

I am momentarily speechless as he stands before me in nothing but a towel wrapped around his waist. He is FINE. I mean, Adam is handsome, but Doctor D is sexy. His frame is lean but not skinny. His arms are well defined, and his muscles flex with his movements. I have never been into tattoos, but the art covering his chest draws my attention. I can't see what he is packing, but if it's like the rest of him I might enjoy this.

Alejandro

I purposely take my time getting undressed and freshen up. I can tell Yara is nervous, so hopefully, some time alone in the spa room will help her calm down. I decide not to put on any clothes after my shower. I keep the king-sized towel wrapped around my waist and head back downstairs. I don't knock on the door to the spa room; I just enter. Yara jumps like a scared rabbit and grabs her dress to put in front of her.

"What's wrong?" I ask her as I enter and close the door. She is taking me in from my head to my toes. I can tell she likes what she sees, but she does not answer my question.

"Yara?"

"Yes?"

"What's wrong?"

"Oh um, I was looking for a sheet or something to cover me while on the table."

"You won't need a sheet for this massage." She looks at me perplexed. "I'm going to see all of you and touch all of you."

I remove the dress from her hands and place it on the hanger. Her body is nice and toned. She has smaller breasts like a B cup, but they are full and remind me of mangoes. She has a nice Brazilian wax on her pussy. Her legs are toned, and her toenails are painted a soft blue-gray color which I find different. I would have guessed red. I take her hand and help her get on the massage table. I stare into her eyes and gently caress her face.

"Please lay down face first." She looks at me with hesitancy.

"Yara, I will not hurt you. I want to relax you and learn what stimulates you."

She lies down on her stomach. I lower the lights and turn on the lavender oil diffuser. I run my hands lightly down her back, across her ass and down her legs. I take her right foot and knead it like dough. She lets out a soft moan, and damn, it's sexy. I do the same to her left foot. I massage her from her feet to her back. I rub some warm oil on my hands and start to massage her slowly. I love massaging her ass. It's not too big or small, she has the perfect ass with nice juicy cheeks. I wonder if she has ever had her ass eaten. I lean over and kiss each of her ass cheeks. I inhale her spicy scent.

The Surrogate

The little moans she makes while I rub her has my dick at attention and ready to slide in between her thighs. As I massage her neck, I squeeze just a lit bit harder and press on the base of her skull. Her body relaxes as she bites her lip and moans. I smell her arousal and glide my hands down her back and in between her legs. I slide two fingers into her pussy and stroke her button.

"Oh my God", she moans as she cums all over my fingers. I remove my fingers from her and help her turn over.

Her cinnamon-colored nipples are hard and begging to be sucked. I pour more oil on my hands and proceed to tease her nipples, making them harder. I can't resist, so I take one into my mouth and give it a suck. Yara's eyes open in surprise. I release the nipple and continue to massage her body, touching her everywhere, except for her pussy. I wipe my hands on a towel and pull open the drawer to grab a feather. I run the feather up the soles of her feet and her legs. I move the feather lightly up her legs, stroking them, sometimes drawing circles. Her breathes are coming faster the closer I move towards her pussy. I run the feather over the top of her mound and between her legs. I open her legs wider and play with her pussy with the feather. Her pussy lips are wet. I take my thumb and massage her clit to come out and play. Once it is standing at attention, I rub the feather over it and continue to massage it with my thumb. She tries to still my hands, but I admonish her.

"Let that pussy cum." I spread her legs wider and pull her down to the middle of the table and give her pussy a long lick. She opens her pussy, and it's like a beautiful waterfall the way it is glistening. I stiffen my tongue and lick her pussy until she cums. Harsh moans leave her lips. I raise from between her legs and run my hands up her body to massage her breasts.

The Surrogate

"Tell me what you want, Yara."

She looks me in my eyes and says, "I want you to fuck me and make me cum again."

I lower the massage bed and command her to get on her hands and knees." I drop the towel from around my waist. My dick is cement hard and leaking. I stroke it from the bottom of my shaft to the head, spreading the precum all over it. Yara looks at me then at my dick. "Get on your hands and knees." She slowly complies.

Yara with her ass in the air is something to see. Her asshole is glistening from her pussy leaking. I want to rim her asshole. Instead, I grab her hips and blow on her pussy. I massage her ass as I slowly slide my thick mushroomed head into her pussy and push my length inside her slick channel. Shit, she feels good. How can she be this tight? I slide my dick out and push back into her center a few times trying to stretch her so she can take all of me. I pound into her hard and deep. She falls forward on the table. I grab her hips and pull her back to my dick. I stroke her pussy with long sure strokes. I chant her name like I'm praying to a deity. No pussy has ever gripped me like hers. She is moaning loudly and throwing her ass back.

"Yes, just like that, she screams."

"Play with your clit so you can cum all over me. I want to feel you drown my dick with your sweet pussy."

Yara slides her fingers down to her pussy, and I increase the tempo. We are both moaning. I feel her pussy getting wetter and tighter and know she is close. I swivel my hips, and her pussy puts my dick in a choke hold.

"Yara, I'm about to cum. Cum with me baby." A few more strokes and we cum together on a yell of each other's name. I pull my dick out and cum all over her ass. I push my fingers in her pussy and stroke her while she is still trembling from her orgasm. I roll my thumb over her clit and finger her pussy. She responds, so I add a third finger and push deep in her pussy. She is so stimulated it doesn't take long before she cums again. I remove my fingers and lick her juices as she watches me with a contented smile on her face.

Yara

I just had the most amazing orgasms. I feel like I'm high. I feel like a fat cat who has been rubbed into contentment. I also feel sad because Adam can't make me feel this way.

"You faked it with your ex-husband. Why?"

"I don't want to talk about him," I respond.

Damn it. Why does he have to ruin the mood by asking about sex with my ex? Who does that? I just want to enjoy the multiple orgasms he's given me. I am lying on the massage table and now I want to go. I hop off so I can get dressed to leave. Doctor D watches me get dressed with eyes that assess my every move.

"How do you know I faked it with Adam?"

"Because you didn't hesitate to do what I told you to do during sex. There was nothing frigid about sex with you. The orgasms you had with me weren't fake."

"I faked it with Adam because he was never attentive to my needs, not like this. When I would tell him to slow down or that I didn't like a certain position, he would make it seem like I was demanding in bed. After a while, I gave up trying to get him to understand and just went through the motions. I loved him, and he just threw our marriage away because I couldn't satisfy him, when the truth is, he couldn't satisfy me. To make it worse, he told all his male friends that I was a lousy lay. I run a multi-million-dollar company but can't satisfy my husband."

I am in tears as the pain and rejection of my marriage ending, and not being good enough for Adam rush out. Dr. D pulls me into his arms and holds me while I cry. He lifts my face from his chest and looks me in the eyes. He kisses me with a passion that makes my heart ache. I angle my head so I can taste all of his lips. His tongue invades my mouth, and we kiss like horny teenagers to long lost loves. I feel like he is telling me secrets with this kiss. I pull away, and his gray eyes are dark and stormy. Just as he is about to say something my phone goes off, signaling the end of our session.

Alejandro

Kissing Yara is everything a kiss should be. Her lips are soft and meet mine in a duel to see who would lose their breath first. I tangle my hand in her hair and devour her mouth, or is she devouring me. I have never felt this attracted to a client. Yara pulls away from our kiss, and just as I open my mouth to ask her to stay and have dinner with me the alarm on her phone rings. The ringing brings me back to reality, and I shake my head. She is a client, and I don't have personal relationships with clients.

I help her get dressed and walk her to the door. "Thank you for this. Thank you for making me feel." I kiss her lips again and smile at her.

"The pleasure was all mine, Yara. Call me if you want another session."

I see the light in her eyes dim a little bit, but she smiles and says okay. I know that I won't see her again once she leaves, and I feel some type of way about it. I have never crossed the line with clients, but there is something about her that makes me want to love her and be loved by her.

Alejandro - Three months later

I saw Yara today. She was having lunch with her ex. Why did my chest get tight?

Client 5 – Laila

Alejandro

Laila is a 28-year-old administrative assistant at a law firm downtown. She came to me because she wants to explore her voyeuristic tendencies.

Laila

It started by accident.

I left work and went grocery shopping only to realize that I did not have my wallet. Fuck my life! I would have to leave all my items and go back to work to get it. I had no money and no license. I was riding dirty.

I rushed back to my desk to get my wallet when I hear what sounded like a moan coming from Mr. Mansfield's office. I stand mannequin still when I hear it again, definitely moaning. I didn't know what was happening, if he was ill or what. I head towards his door to knock when I hear not just one person moaning but two. Oh my God, who is he having sex with? The right thing to do would have been to leave, but nope, I'm nosy. I open the door on the guise of checking on him, but I was not ready to see him fucking the shit out of the HR manager Karen. I mean, he is pounding into her pussy like it stole something from him. I stand there transfixed and turned on watching my boss fuck. I don't know how long I watch, but her screaming her release broke me from my spell, and I quickly closed the door and got the hell out of there.

The Surrogate

I can't believe I caught my boss fucking in the office. I was turned the fuck on. Groceries were forgotten as I made it home, stripped down, and proceeded to fuck myself to completion. The next day I went to work like I saw nothing. I wasn't going to say anything to my boss about what I saw. Right before lunch, he calls me into his office.

"Tell me, Laila, did you enjoy watching me fuck?"

I school my face and respond, "I don't know what you are talking about."

"Sure you don't. I saw you watching me yesterday when you shouldn't have been here. Tell me, did you like how I fucked Karen? Did hearing us turn you on? I bet you went home and fucked yourself, didn't you?"

I stood there speechless and so fucking turned on by his words. "I don't mind you watching, but if you watch me then I get to watch you." My mouth falls open, and I stare at him in shock.

"What?"

"If you watch me then I get to watch you."

I reply back to him that he is mistaken, and I don't know what he is talking about. He looks me dead in the face and replies, "Then you are fired." I stand there in shock not believing what he said. "Listen, I won't say anything to anyone about what I saw. It's not like I can go to HR."

He chuckles and says, "You are right."

I can't lose my job, so I agree to his proposition. Little did I know this would start an obsession of me needing to watch.

About a month later at the company holiday party, I'm feeling good and tipsy. I walk out of the ballroom to find a bathroom to pee and freshen up. I had been flirting with Brad in accounting, and tonight was looking promising.

I'm in the bathroom and just finished doing my business when the door bursts open. I hear a male voice say check the stalls. I immediately pull my feet up so they can't be seen. The female voice says they are empty, but probably not for long. We need to be quick. I couldn't believe it was happening again. I was afraid to move or breathe hard. They are kissing, and I hear pants being unzipped. I peek through the crack in the stall, and I see HR Karen on her knees sucking my boss's dick. I couldn't see how big it was, but she was putting lips to that shit. All I hear is her slurping and sucking and his moans. Suddenly, he pulls away and tells her to take off her panties and get on the counter. She does, and I see his junk, and damn, he is packing an impressive dick. She hops on the counter, and he spreads her legs and begins to eat her pussy. He was so far in her pussy

I'm sure she gave him a facial. He pulls her to the end of the sink and begins to fuck her. I should have just stayed quiet, and still, but nope, I had to see. I was trying to get a better view of the action by standing on the toilet. Big mistake! My foot slipped into the toilet bowl, and I shrieked. They both hear me. I am busted. Imagine my boss's surprise when he discovers me once again watching him fuck.

"What are you doing in here?" he asks.

"Using the bathroom," I reply.

HR Karen is horrified and trying to put herself back together while my boss just glares at me. Then he smiles wickedly. We will discuss this on Monday. Needless to say, I hightailed it out of the party and went straight home. I fucked myself with my toy and my fingers before drifting off to sleep.

Monday morning I arrive at work fully ready to deny what I saw. I bring Mr. Mansfield his coffee, and to my shock HR Karen is there. Long story short, I was fired and had to sign a non-disclosure agreement not to retaliate. I left with a check for two weeks' pay and all of my accumulated vacation time. I also received three months of severance pay.

Alejandro

"Why are you here, Laila?"

"It's been six months since I was fired, and I am obsessed with watching people have sex."

"You mean, like porn or you watch other people?"

"I tried watching porn, but it's not the same as seeing real people. I can get off to porn, but I have stronger orgasms when I watch people.

"How are you watching people?"

"Through a website where you can watch people having sex."

"How often do you go to the website?"

"At least four times a week, but lately, it's like I can't get enough. The thrill is there, and I get off, but I also feel like I need more."

"More what?"

"More excitement, more intensity."

"Are you looking to make this a permanent kink, or is this something you are exploring and hoping to get out of your system?"

"I want to get this out of my system. I have never been into watching people have sex before the incident with my former boss."

"How would you feel if people watched you have sex?"

"I don't know. I've never thought about it."

The Surrogate

"Meet me at this address at 9:00 pm. on Saturday. Wear a black dress and red high heels. When you arrive, give them this card at the door. Do not be late. I will be waiting for you."

Laila

Dr. D hands me a black card with the words je veux regarder written on it.

"What does this mean?"

"You will see when you arrive."

"Okay."

I arrive at the address with five minutes to spare. The building looks like an old hotel tucked in between old storefronts. I hope I'm in the right place as there is not a lot of traffic in this area. I approach the door and enter the lobby. There is a huge desk made of black marble. Behind the desk is a beautiful Latina woman. She is tall and curvaceous. Her long black hair is straight and flows down her back. She is wearing a black leather bustier that barely contains her tits. The bustier is paired with black leather pants and six-inch heels which makes her look taller than what she is. She is probably 5'5 or 5'6. I approach the desk and hand her the card. She takes the card, looks at me, and gives me a wicked smile. "Welcome, Laila. My name is Maria, and welcome to SEX. Let me escort you to your floor."

I have so many questions. "How do you know my name?"

"You have Alejandro's card, and he secured this experience for you."

"Wait, is he not meeting me here?"

"He is already here and waiting for you. He will explain everything else."

The Surrogate

Maria joins me in the lobby, and we take an elevator to the third floor. We walk down a hallway that has five doors. The last door is #27. She knocks two times, and the door is opened by Dr. D. "Thanks, Maria, for escorting my guest."

"Anytime, you have full access. Ring me if you need anything." She turns and retreats down the hallway.

"Hello, Laila. How are you this evening?"

"I'm a little confused. She called this place SEX. Why am I here?"

You are here tonight to get your fill of watching people fuck and to let people watch you get off."

"Wait, I never agreed to that."

"You will when the time is right. But for now, what would you like to drink, and what would you like to watch? Do you want male/female?

Female/Female? Male/Male? Interracial? Asian? Whatever you desire to watch is available here at SEX."

Doctor D points a remote at the TV and a literal menu pulls up on the screen. I am shocked and excited. I get to create any scenario I want. "You can choose whatever you like. We have several hours of playtime."

Alejandro

I watch the look on Laila's face. She is so turned on just by choosing what she wants. "Laila, think of this as a dinner menu. You can start with an appetizer that would be oral, or you can skip to dinner and create whatever combination you want. Dessert will hopefully be you, or you can choose whatever ending you want. When you are done putting in your order, take off your dress and join me in the next room."

The room I have chosen is decorated in red and black. The bed is a four-poster black bed with a red headboard. The shelves on either side of the bed are full of all types of toys. I have also chosen dildos in sizes from six to ten inches. There are several types of rabbits and bullets. The other wall holds a wet bar. I take off my clothes and put on a custom black silk robe. About fifteen minutes later, Laila comes into the room. Her eyes widen when she sees the bed and the toys.

Would you like something to drink?

Yes, some water please, and a dirty martini if you have it.

"I'm curious to see what you have chosen for us this evening."

"For us? Yes, I will guide you through this experience."

She starts to look a little nervous. "Do not worry, Laila. I am here to help you achieve ultimate pleasure. You don't have to do anything you don't want to. When you are tired of watching just point the remote and close the window."

"The window?"

"Yes, in about ten minutes that curtain will open, and your menu will begin. Let's get that drink and get in bed."

Laila gets in the bed, and soon the lights in the room dim and the curtain opens. I have no idea what she has chosen but imagine my surprise when it's two women.

The first woman is black, and the second woman is white. The black woman is Selene, and the white woman is Katelyn. They both have large breasts and clean-shaven pussies. They enter the room and begin to kiss. Selene lies down on the bed and spreads her pussy wide. Katelyn drops to her knees and French kisses her pussy.

The Surrogate

Selene is moaning and fucking Katelyn's face. Katelyn slides up Selene's body, and they kiss and get into the 69 position.

Laila is watching intently and playing with her breasts. I say nothing as I watch her pleasure herself. Soon, her breathing changes to panting, and she is fingering her pussy. All three women are moaning, and just as Selene sticks her tongue in Katelyn's asshole, Laila cums. Selene and Katelyn are still going at it, so I remove Laila's panties and spread her legs wider. "Play with your pussy again. Don't stop until they cum."

I can hear how wet Laila's pussy is. A few minutes later Selene and Katelyn climax. Selene's pussy is wide open for us to see her cream gush out. Katelyn greedily licks all of it, and Laila cums again. I prolong her orgasm by sucking on her hardened nipples and pushing her fingers deeper in her drenched pussy. When I feel her body relaxing, I remove her fingers and suck them clean. She looks at me with eyes blazing with desire. We kiss, and she strokes my dick through my robe.

"Are you ready to see more?"

Laila

I have watched a lot of people, but seeing them live in front of me, hearing them moan, and seeing their orgasms was downright sexy. My body is on fire, and I am ready for the next item on the menu. For my dinner, I chose a Latina woman and two men. The woman is Marisol, and her partners tonight are Antonio and Colton. Marisol has the biggest breasts I've ever seen. They are big like melons and have dusky rose-colored nipples. Her pussy is clean shaven. Antonio has long dark hair pulled into a ponytail and an impressive seven-inch penis with a slight curve. Colton has brown hair cut low. His penis is seven inches and thick. Since Marisol is taking on two men, I didn't want to kill her with guys who have monster dicks. The curtain opens and all three are on the bed. Marisol is in the middle being kissed and fondled by both men. Colton tosses her left leg over his and fingers her pussy. Both men are sucking her breasts. She spreads her legs wider so Colton can slide another finger in her pussy while Antonio thumbs her clit.

She is moaning loudly, and her pussy is wet. I'm stroking Dr. D's dick, when suddenly, I see Marisol's pussy cum and drench both guys' fingers. Antonio crawls between her legs to gobble up her essence. Colton fucks her mouth with his dick. Dr. D crawls between my legs and starts to eat my pussy. I moan and rock my hips faster towards his face. I'm close to cumming when Antonio slides his dick inside Marisol's dripping wet pussy. The sounds Marisol makes sends me off, and I cum down Dr. D's throat. He continues to lick me until I push his head away. He kisses inside my thighs.

We watch as Colton and Antonio get Marisol into a new position. She straddles Colton and starts to ride his dick. Antonio is on his knees behind her playing with her breasts. He pushes her forward so that she is chest to chest with Colton. I can see her bouncing up and down off his dick. I see her juices clinging to his shaft every time she comes up on his dick. Antonio licks his thumb and rubs it around her asshole. She moans and slows down her ride on Colton's dick. Antonio sticks his tongue in her ass, and Marisol screams in pleasure. Antonio eats her ass while Marisol rides Colton.

Alejandro

The Surrogate

Laila is dripping wet. She is glued to the sight of Antonio eating Marisol's ass. I slide two fingers into her pussy and stroke her slowly. She moans and grabs the sheets.

"Do you like that?"

"Yes," she moans on a shaky breath. I continue to play with her.

Meanwhile, Antonio is sliding his dick in Marisol's ass. Laila makes a sound between a gasp and a moan. I watch her watch as Marisol gets pounded from the front and back. Laila starts to ride my fingers. I grab a dildo and slide it in her pussy along with my two fingers. Laila gushes all over the toy and my fingers. She tries to close her legs, but I keep them open and continue to fuck her greedy pussy with the dildo. Her juices leak out of her. Her pussy is so wet and pink. Her clit is puffed up and begging to be played with. In the window, Marisol is now on her side and Colton is fucking her in the ass. Antonio is licking her pussy. He finds her clit and flicks his tongue over it. Marisol and Colton cum at the same time. He pulls out, and Marisol gets on her knees to swallow his cum. Antonio is jacking his dick watching as she licks Colton clean. I'm jacking my dick as I watch Laila pull the dildo out and put it in her mouth to suck it. Antonio's dick is so hard as he grabs Marisol's head and slides his dick in her mouth. She is deepthroating his dick while Colton eats her pussy. All I hear are the moans of Marisol and the guys. Laila is watching me jack my dick. She leans over and wraps her lips around my head and sucks. I grab her head and proceed to fuck her mouth like Antonio is doing to Marisol. Laila takes me all the way to the back of her throat. I'm close to cumming when Antonio shoots his load down Marisol's throat, and I soon follow. We lay on the bed and try to catch our breath. The curtain closes, and the room grows darker.

The Surrogate

Laila

We must have dozed off. I wake up feeling relaxed and ready for my dessert. Dr. D. is laying on his back. His thick dick is half hard and begging for me to suck it. I press the remote so that the curtain opens and straddle Doctor D's lap to lick the head of his juicy dick. He stirs on a moan. I tell him it's time for dessert. He moans and runs his fingers through my hair.

"What's for dessert?"

"Me. I'm going to fuck you while Selene, Marisol, and Katelyn watch."

It was empowering to see the surprised look on his face. We both look up when we hear moans coming from the ladies watching us. I deep throat as much of his dick as I can. He is moaning and fucking my mouth hard. He is hard as steel. I pop him from my mouth and straddle his dick. It feels like it's triple the size inside my pussy. I slide up and down slowly to get accustomed to the size. He grabs my breasts as I start my ride. I'm getting a good motion going when he rubs his thumb over my clit. I moan and do a Kegel on his dick. I lean back so I can take more of his dick and give him better access to my clit. I'm riding him fast, and his thumb on my clit sets off my orgasm. He leans up and holds me tight while he fucks me from the bottom. All I can hear is the slap of my ass hitting his thighs. He slows his pace to turns me around so I can face the screen giving the ladies a better view of his dick tunneling into my pussy.

"Come for me again, Laila." He slides his fingers over my slippery folds.

The image on the screen is hot. Marisol is eating Selene's pussy, and Katelyn is eating out Marisol. We all watch each other. I am about to explode when Dr. D slides a finger into my ass. I yell. "Yes, fuck my ass!"

I grind my pussy on his dick as Selene's pussy squirts. Katelyn's pussy is dripping as Selene and Marisol tag team her. They lick her pussy at the same time. It's so hot seeing two tongues in one pussy that I explode all over of Dr. D's dick. He cums a moment later deep inside my pussy. The combination of my juices and his cum is dripping all over my thighs and on his dick, but he holds me tight until he stops twitching in my pussy. He pulls out, and we watch as Selene and Marisol make Katelyn cum. I lay next to Dr. D exhausted but satisfied.

Alejandro

Laila and I lay in bed and kiss after watching the ladies get each other off. I stroke her breasts and slide one finger into her pussy.

I ask her, "Have you had enough for tonight?"

"Yes, I am well satisfied. I don't think I will need to watch for awhile. All of my fantasies happened tonight."

"Good. Let's end with one more orgasm."

I pull her to the end of the bed and proceed to lick her pussy. I spot the dildo we used earlier and slide it in her pussy.

"Fuck yourself while I eat your ass." Laila bucks her hips as soon as I put my tongue in her ass. I push her legs over her head, and she works her pussy with the toy. I eat her ass then insert two fingers into her tight hole.

Laila

The Surrogate

Oh shit, I'm so full. His tongue in my ass feels so good. I feel myself shatter into a million pieces when I feel him slide his fingers into my ass. The pressure is too much. My legs are shaking, and I scream like a fucking banshee when I cum. Doctor D takes his tongue and fingers out of my ass and removes the toy. He climbs up my body and places his dick in my mouth. I suck and lick his dick until he cums down my throat and spills out of my mouth. We are both hot, sweaty, and spent. After a brief nap we take a shower and get dressed. It's 2:00 am when we leave SEX. It was the best sexual experience of my life and worth every damn dollar.

The End

L. NICOLE

The Surrogate

Author Thank You

This novella would not be possible without the help of so many people.

This book is dedicated to Author Sonja B. because she posted the picture of the sexy man that became my muse for this story. Thank you, Sonja, for encouraging me to write and for answering my numerous questions. You are an amazing author and friend.

Carolee Samuda and RK Renton, thank you for encouraging me to write the damn book, sis!

To babe, thanks for going along with my crazy idea to write. Thank you for your love and support.

To my #1 fan, my mom Gladys Winston. Thank you for cheering me on and being my best friend. I love you to the moon and back.

To my sistahs Nicole and Olga who suffered through me reading a chapter of this out loud. Thank you for the laughs and the encouragement.

L. NICOLE

Thank you to Creative Design Concepts for the amazing cover. Thank you, Pam Gonzales, with Love2ReadRomance for the editing. I am extremely grateful to you because I had so many questions about editing and you patiently answered and helped me along the way. You are simply the best!

Thank you to every single person who will read this book, leave a review, share the link or post about it. I can't say thank you enough. Thank you to the ladies in the read this book chat room, y'all are awesome.

Last but never least, Thank You, God, for this amazing journey.

Social Media

Email: readthisbook@hotmail.com

Facebook:

https://www.facebook.com/groups/41967317565

3434

The Surrogate

Instagram:

www.instagram.com/readthisbooklr

Printed in Great Britain
by Amazon

51459084R00075